The Rescuers

Twin Books

LONGMEADOW
PRESS

The United Nations building stands proudly among the skyscrapers of New York. Inside its walls, delegates from all over the world come to talk, and talk, and talk!

They talk about ways to bring peace to the world. In vast conference halls, they talk long into the night about how to put an end to all wars. But while the delegates are busy upstairs, something very important is happening in the basement.

How amazed the delegates would have been if they had seen what was happening down below one morning. The International Rescue Aid Society was in emergency session.

"Delegates," the Chairman began, "you have been summoned from all corners of the globe because we have reason to believe that someone is in distress. As you know, our society has never failed to answer a call for help."

That very day, a bottle had been found in New York harbor, and it contained a message.

The Rescue Aid Society members had been convened to deal with the problem. The last member to arrive was Miss Bianca, a kind and beautiful lady mouse who had come all the way from Hungary.

"Take a seat, Miss Bianca,"
said a French delegate. "Now
that you are here, we can open
the bottle."

The mice had a problem: how were they going to get the message out of the enormous bottle? An old comb soon became a ladder.

A fellow named Bernard, who was a sort of handymouse, was appointed to climb up, remove the cork from the bottle and pull out the message.

Getting up the ladder was easy, but the neck of the bottle was very slippery, and the cork was firmly stuck.

"Bravo, Bernard! Bravo!" called Bianca. Hearing her, Bernard tugged harder. *Pop!* The cork flew out of the bottle. The message was quickly pulled out and unfolded.

Miss Bianca read the message, which was faint and water-spotted. "To Morningside Orphanage, New York. I am in terrible trouble. Help. Penny."

"Poor child," the Chairman Mouse sighed. "How can we ever find her? It certainly won't be easy."

"Mr. Chairman, may I have this assignment?" asked Bianca.

"Why, Miss Bianca!" exclaimed the Chairman. "You are a woman. You could never . . . but . . . well, at least take a co-agent with you."

Bianca pointed to Bernard. "I choose Mr. Bernard," she said.

Bernard was so surprised that he almost fainted!

That very night, Bernard and Bianca were on Penny's trail. Sheltered from the rain, they pored over a map.

"Morningside Orphanage," said Bernard, pointing. "Here it is. Three blocks down and four blocks over."

Moments later, Bernard and Bianca came to a halt outside a big, dark house. The sign on the creaky, old gate said:
MORNINGSIDE
ORPHANAGE
There were no lights in the windows. Everyone was asleep.

As they ran up the steps, Bernard nervously warned Bianca to be very careful. They quickly slid under the locked door and began their search.

"Psst. Miss Bianca, over here," Bernard whispered. "I found somethin'."

Bernard had found a box with the word "Penny" scratched on the side. "These are Penny's belongings," he said.

"Good work," Bianca whispered. "Now we're getting somewhere."

Just then a big cat with a droopy moustache sidled up to them. "Now, looky here, you two. I'm a mite too old to be chasin' mice. So tell me—what are you searching for?"

Bernard and Bianca just knew they could trust the cat, whose name was Rufus, and were soon telling him all about their search for Penny.

Rufus knew Penny
well. "I loved that little
girl. The last time I saw
her, she was sittin' on her
bed all alone, sad 'cause no one wanted
to adopt her. She just cried and cried, and clung to her little
teddy bear. I told her to have faith, but . . . well, the next
thing I heard, Penny was gone."

Bernard was shocked, and asked if the cat knew where
Penny might be.

"Well, there's this nasty couple who run a pawn shop down
the street. They tried to kidnap her once," the cat replied.

"Miss Bianca, we must go there and investigate," said
Bernard.

A few moments later, the
curious mice found themselves
outside a store named
"Medusa's Pawn Shop." The
shop was closed, so they
slipped quietly under the door.

Suddenly, the phone rang! Bernard and Bianca hid in the shadows as a cruel-looking woman with bright red hair and long fingernails snatched the telephone.

"Medusa's Pawn Shop . . . hello, Snoops . . . have you found the diamond yet? Give you more time? You bungler! Bottles? You found Penny sending messages in bottles? Can't you control a little girl? I am taking the next flight down to Devil's Bayou!"

Medusa rushed out to her car and sped away to the airport.

"Quick," said Bernard. "She must be heading for the airport. Let's hurry!" But by the time the mice got there, Medusa had left.

"Look, Bernard, what's that sign over there?" asked Bianca.

"Fly Albatross Airlines," read Bernard.

The friends rushed into the control tower, and Bernard headed straight for the microphone.

A voice was calling over the control tower's radio. "Albatross Flight 13 to tower. Am I clear to land?"

Bernard leaned into the microphone and said, "You have *our* permission to land."

Suddenly a huge, white albatross in a cap and goggles swooped down unsteadily, and landed with a thud.

"Hello, friends. Just call me Orville," he said. "Fit as a fiddle and ready to hit the wild blue yonder!"

Bernard wasn't so sure. Watching Orville dust himself off, he said to Bianca, "Maybe we'd better take the train."

"The train!" exclaimed Bianca. "Why, Bernard, surely you're not a 'fraidy-cat!"

"Fraidy-cat?" asked Bernard. "It's just that . . . I like trains." But not wishing to appear cowardly in front of Bianca, he smiled and climbed aboard Orville with her. He told Orville to fly them to Devil's Bayou.

"Fasten your seat belts," said Orville.

"Be sure that your belt is fastened tight," Bernard said to Bianca.

"Yes Bernard, dear," Bianca answered, as Orville prepared to take off.

"I sure wish we'd have taken the train," Bernard muttered.

Meanwhile, in a land of swirling mists and deep, dangerous swamps, a little girl was running from a shipwrecked riverboat. In her hand was a little brown teddy bear.

"Penny!" There was only one woman in the whole world with such a voice.

"That little brat has escaped again," snarled Medusa. She came out of the riverboat with two crocodiles, Brutus and Nero. "Bring her back, boys," she ordered.

Brutus and Nero licked their chops. They were two very hungry crocodiles. They slid into the swamp in search of poor Penny.

The furious Medusa jumped into a very strange-looking contraption. It coughed and sputtered and kicked smoke into the air. Medusa rode it deep into the swamp to search for Penny.

Just then, Orville was flying over the swamp with Bernard and Bianca on his back. Having reached their destination, the two mice jumped off the albatross and fell through the murky air.

Using Bianca's umbrella as a parachute, they floated downward and landed with a bump.

Two of Orville's friends, Luke and Ellie Mae, had seen them fall and came running to meet them. Ellie Mae reached them first.

Bianca was just about to explain everything to Ellie Mae and Luke. But then Nero and Brutus loomed out of the swamp carrying a girl and her teddy bear.

"That must be Penny," Bianca exclaimed. "We've got to find out where they're taking her."

Ellie Mae said, "You'll need a boat. Evinrude's got the fastest boat around here."

Evinrude was a dragonfly. His boat was a leaf that he propelled from behind. He pushed Bernard and Bianca through the water as they followed Brutus and Nero.

"Faster, Evinrude," Bianca said.

They were soon skimming so fast through the swamp, they lost sight of Brutus and Nero.

"Slow down," Bernard said. "They've got to be around here somewhere." Evinrude pulled back on the leaf-boat to slow it down.

"Come on," said Bianca to Bernard. "Let's head for that riverboat. I'm sure that's where the crocodiles are taking Penny."

Bianca was right!

The mice thanked Evinrude and asked him to wait for them. Then they crept silently aboard the ship to search for Penny.

"Ssshhh! Listen!" Bianca whispered. "I can hear a man's voice."

"It must be that Snoops character Medusa was yelling at over the phone," said Bernard. "Let's get a little closer."

The two mice peered through a window.

"So you tried to run away. Well, it didn't work, did it?" asked Snoops. "Now, you behave, or I'll let Brutus and Nero have your old teddy bear."

"You will not!" Penny shouted.

"Don't you sass me," Snoops said. "Boys, take this naughty girl to her room."

Penny and her precious teddy bear had just been locked away when the wicked Medusa burst through the door.

"Where is she?" screamed Medusa, her eyes flashing like knives. "Where is she, you bungler!"

"Where . . . where is she?" stammered a very nervous Snoops. "I sent her up to her room."

Medusa flew up the stairs three at a time, then paused outside of Penny's door. "If I'm nice to Penny, maybe she'll do as I ask," thought the woman slyly.

"Penny dear!" Medusa called from behind the door. "Do you know what would make Auntie Medusa very happy?"

"You want me to find that diamond," Penny answered. "But I tried as hard as I could, honest. And I've found a lot of other things."

"Yes, you stupid child!" exclaimed Medusa, bursting into the room impatiently. "But not the Devil's Eye. That's the one I want!"

Bernard and Bianca had been listening from under a table. They were watching Medusa so carefully that they didn't notice who was slithering towards them.

"Uh-oh," Bernard said. "Bianca, they smell your perfume."

Bernard and Bianca sped across the room, but Brutus and Nero were close behind.

There was a huge old pipe organ standing by a wall. Bernard and Bianca quickly scampered inside.

As soon as they entered the organ,
Bernard and Bianca hid inside one of
the pipes. The crocodiles continued to
search for them, and the mice were
terribly frightened when Brutus's angry
eye peered into their pipe.

With a malicious smile, Brutus sat at the keyboard and began to play. The air in the pipes started to swirl as the organ let out a deafening screech. The wind puffing through the organ bounced Bernard and Bianca in and out of the pipes as though they were ping-pong balls. Nero tried to grab them as they popped out.

Fortunately for the two friends, Medusa soon put a stop to the crocodiles' noisy concert. She said it gave her a headache. And when all was quiet again, Bernard and Bianca were able to scurry away.

The friends scampered up to Penny's window ledge. The girl was praying by her bed.

The two mice quietly slipped into Penny's room as she prayed, "Dear God, please let someone find my bottle . . . because running away isn't working. Amen."

Bianca gently tapped on Penny's hand.

"Where'd you come from?" asked the astonished girl.

"We found the bottle with your message," Bernard answered, "and we've come to rescue you."

Penny asked, "Did you bring somebody big with you, like the police?"

"Ah . . . no," Bernard admitted.

"But if the three of us work together and have a little faith . . ." Bianca began.

". . . things will turn out right," Penny finished.

Together, they began to make a plan.

Later, Bernard found Evinrude, and told him, "Evinrude, we need help. Go get Ellie Mae, and hurry!"

Evinrude sped away.

Bernard hoped that help would arrive in time, and set to work on the next part of the plan.

Suddenly, he heard Medusa's voice. She and Snoops were coming to get Penny.

Bernard and Bianca quickly hid in Penny's pocket so that they could go where she did.

Medusa and Snoops took Penny out to a dark cave. Its entrance was too small for Medusa or Snoops, but Penny could just fit into it.

Medusa grabbed Penny's teddy bear and shoved the girl toward the cave. "You get down there and find that diamond," she shouted, "or you will never see this teddy bear again!"

Penny was lowered into the icy cold cavern. Bernard and Bianca climbed out of her pocket so that they could help her.

Penny told them that pirates used to hide stolen jewels in the cave. One of these jewels was the famous Devil's Eye—but she hadn't been able to find it. Perhaps the pirates had hidden it inside or beneath something.

Just then they saw a glint of light shining from inside an old skull.

Bernard and Bianca climbed inside the skull.

"Holy mackerel," said Bernard. "That's it."

"The Devil's Eye," Bianca agreed.

But the skull was stuck in the ground, and the diamond was too big to fit through the skull's eyes or nose. How could they get it out?

Suddenly Penny had an idea.
During her visits to the cavern,
she had discovered an old
sword. It would be just the
thing to pry open the skull.

Penny slipped the sword between the skull's teeth and pulled with all her might.

"What's taking so long?" Medusa cried. "You get that diamond, or you'll never see daylight again!"

Meanwhile, Penny felt her shoes fill with water. The tide was coming in!

The skull's jaw popped open. Penny grabbed the diamond.

Penny scrambled back into
the bucket, and so did Bernard
and Bianca. Once again, they
hid in her pocket. As
Snoops pulled them up,
Medusa urged him,
"Faster! Faster!"

"Oh, at last! The Devil's Eye—filled with power for its owner," cried Medusa. "And it's all mine!"

"Why, half of it is mine, you double-crossing crook," Snoops said quickly.

Medusa dashed toward the boat, with Snoops running close behind. Brutus, who had followed Medusa to the cave, picked Penny up and followed Medusa and Snoops. In the confusion, Bernard and Bianca slipped away.

Meanwhile, Evinrude had finally reached Luke and Ellie Mae. The two swamp mice rallied their friends to help Penny, Bernard and Bianca. They came charging toward Medusa's riverboat.

At the riverboat, they met Bernard and Bianca, who led the swamp folk up the gangplank. The first thing to do was take care of the crocodiles, and Bernard and Bianca had a plan for doing that.

And what a plan it was!

In the riverboat was a huge, iron elevator. The elevator had bars like a cage. Bianca squirted some of her perfume at the elevator, and the crocodiles headed straight for it, as they had done before.

"Now!" Bernard shouted, and the swamp folk lowered the elevator onto the crocodiles. Now Brutus and Nero were no longer a threat.

It was time to deal with Medusa.

Medusa had Penny and Snoops cornered. Only Penny was brave enough to speak.

"Give me my teddy bear. You promised," Penny insisted.

"Teddy goes with me, my dear," Medusa answered. "I've become quite attached to him." She began to back out of the room. "Follow me, and I'll blast you with this shotgun!"

Elsewhere on the boat, the swamp folk had found
some fireworks, which Snoops sometimes shot into
the sky to signal to Medusa during her trips deep
into the swamps.

Luke and Ellie Mae lit the fuses of the fireworks.

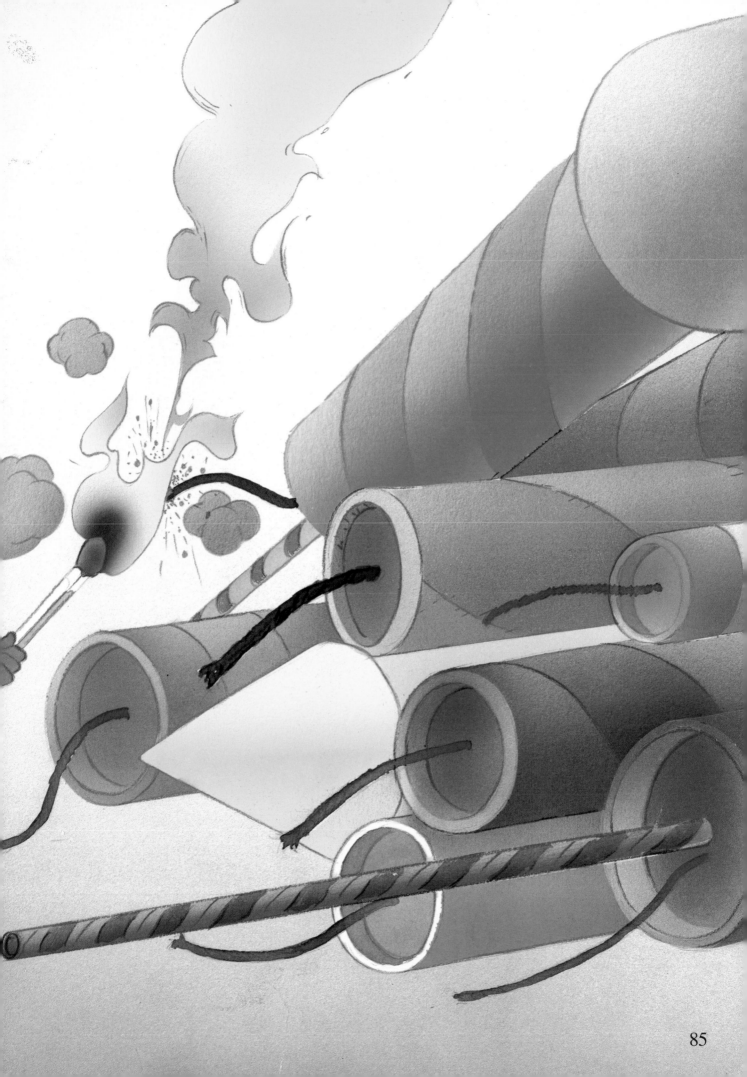

Medusa was still backing away from Penny and Snoops as Bernard and Bianca stretched a wire across the doorway behind her.

As they had planned, the wire tripped Medusa, and she fell backwards. Her gun went *bang*, the fireworks exploded into the air, and Penny's teddy bear flew out of Medusa's hand.

When the bear hit the floor, the seam on its tummy split, revealing the Devil's Eye! Snoops ran to grab it, but Penny was quicker. She ran outside with her teddy bear, following Bernard and Bianca.

The whole gang clambered aboard Medusa's swamp boat.
Penny started it up, and it chugged noisily across the swamp.
Everyone on the swamp boat happily waved goodbye as
the exploding fireworks began to sink the riverboat.

It wasn't a pretty sight. Snoops was bobbing in the water, and, as for Medusa, she clung tightly to a smokestack, protesting loudly about her lost diamond.

"We did it, Bianca," Bernard said.

"Bernard, you were wonderful," Bianca sighed.

Back at the International Rescue Aid Society, their mission accomplished, Bernard and Bianca were given a hero's welcome.

On the Society's television, the members watched the news of the rescue.

"Because of a courageous little girl named Penny, the Devil's Eye is now in the Smithsonian," the announcer said.

Bernard and Bianca smiled as Penny appeared on the screen with her new mother and father. "But what's even more important," the announcer added, "is that this orphan's dream has come true. Today, she is being adopted."

But even at such a happy moment, Penny didn't forget her new friends.

"I didn't do it all by myself. Two little mice from the International Rescue Aid Society, they helped me," she added.

Nobody on the screen believed a word. But Bernard and Bianca didn't mind. For, thanks to Penny, they had found each other, and many adventures lay ahead for these brave rescuers.

This edition produced for
Longmeadow Press
by Twin Books Corp

ISBN 0-681-41429-4

Printed in Hong Kong